THE WOLF
AND THE FOX
AF373618

ONCE UPON A TIME, THERE WAS A WOLF
AND A FOX WHO LIVED IN THE FOREST.

BECAUSE HE WAS STRONGER, THE WOLF BOSSED
THE FOX AROUND, WHO WAS VERY AFRAID OF THE
WICKED ONE AND DREAMED OF LIVING FREELY,
WITHOUT HAVING TO OBEY ANYONE.

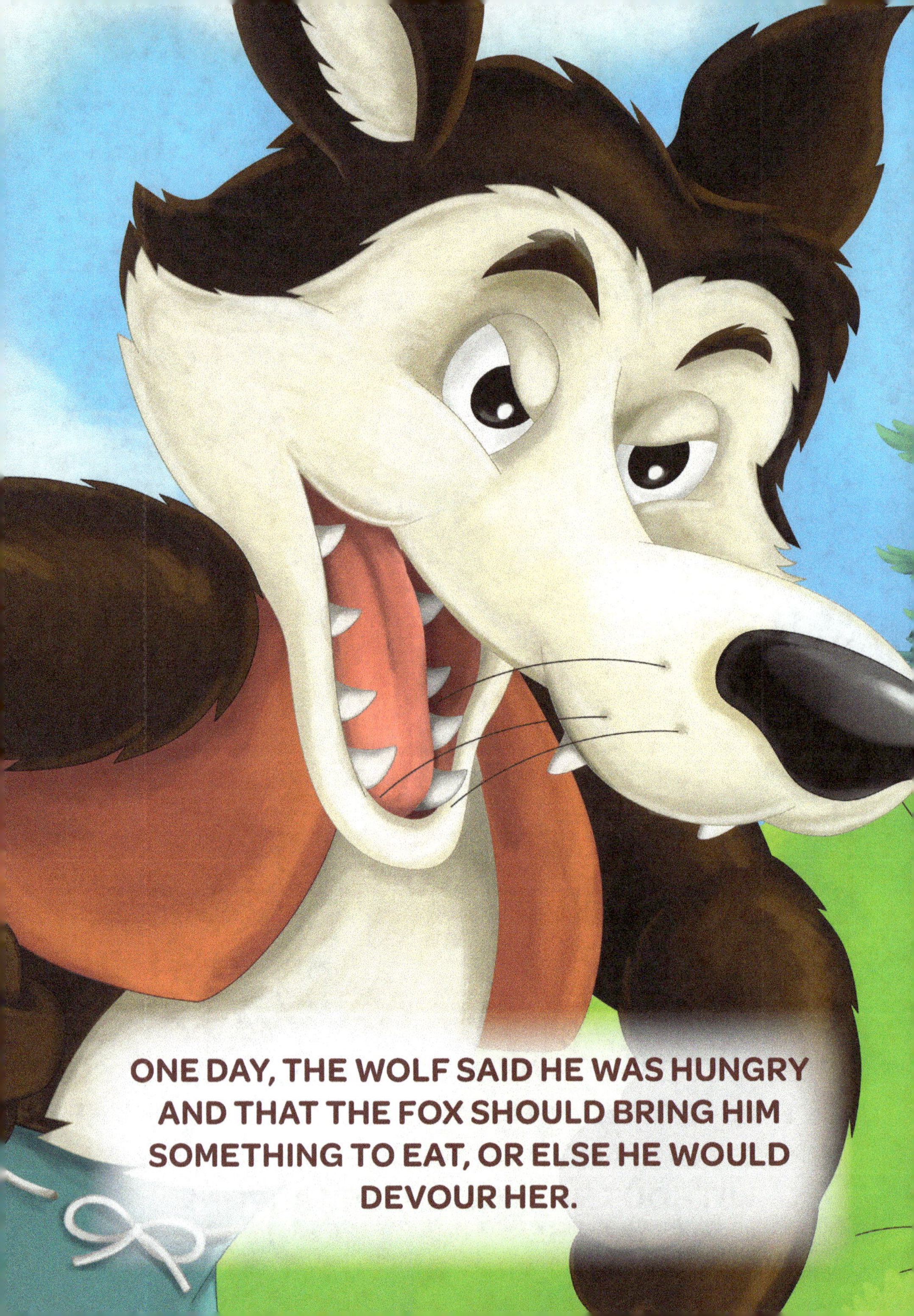
ONE DAY, THE WOLF SAID HE WAS HUNGRY
AND THAT THE FOX SHOULD BRING HIM
SOMETHING TO EAT, OR ELSE HE WOULD
DEVOUR HER.

QUICKLY, THE FOX WENT TO A FARM AND
HUNTED A SHEEP FOR THE WOLF TO HAVE
FOR LUNCH.

AFTER DEVOURING THE ANIMAL, THE WOLF WAS STILL HUNGRY AND DECIDED TO HUNT ANOTHER SHEEP.

HOWEVER, AS HE WAS VERY CLUMSY, HE SCARED THE SHEEP, WHICH RAN AWAY AND STARTED TO BLEAT.

UPON HEARING THE NOISE OF THE ANIMALS,
THE FARMER BECAME WORRIED. WHEN HE SAW
THE WOLF TRYING TO ATTACK HIS SHEEP...

..THE MAN BEAT THE WICKED ONE, MAKING HIM DIZZY.

THE NEXT DAY, THE WOLF FOUND THE FOX
AND AGAIN...

...SAID THAT IF SHE DIDN'T BRING SOMETHING FOR HIM TO EAT, SHE WOULD BE DEVOURED.

THE FOX REMEMBERED THAT EVERY DAY THE OWNER OF A FARM PREPARED DELICIOUS PIES.

SO, SHE WENT TO THE PLACE AND STOLE
A PIE FOR THE WOLF TO DEVOUR.

AFTER LUNCH, THE WOLF DIDN'T FEEL SATISFIED AND DECIDED TO GET ANOTHER PIE.

HOWEVER, BEING VERY CLUMSY,
HE KNOCKED OVER A PITCHER ON THE
KITCHEN FLOOR.

WHEN SHE HEARD THE NOISE, THE FARM OWNER WENT TO THE KITCHEN AND SAW THE WOLF TRYING TO STEAL HER PIES.

THE WOMAN WENT AFTER HIM AND BEAT HIM UP, LEAVING HIM INJURED.

THE NEXT DAY, THE WOLF AGAIN FORCED THE FOX TO FIND SOMETHING FOR HIM TO EAT, THREATENING TO DEVOUR HER.

SO, THE FOX SAID THAT A MAN WHO LIVED NEARBY USED TO HANG PIECES OF MEAT IN HIS KITCHEN AND THAT SHE WOULD GO THERE.

WITHOUT KNOWING HOW THE FOX MANAGED TO STEAL THINGS WITHOUT BEING CAUGHT...

...THE WOLF WANTED TO GO ALONG TO GET MORE MEAT AND LEARN HOW TO ESCAPE WITHOUT GETTING CAUGHT.

WHEN THEY ARRIVED AT THE MAN'S HOUSE,
THEY FOUND SEVERAL PIECES OF MEAT HANGING.

THE FOX AND THE WOLF STARTED TO EAT THEM.
HOWEVER, WHILE THE WOLF GORGED HIMSELF,
THE FOX REMAINED ALERT TO SEE IF THE MAN
WAS ARRIVING.

UPON HEARING A NOISE, THE FOX LEFT THROUGH
THE HOLE THEY HAD ENTERED THE KITCHEN,
FLEEING THE SCENE.

WHILE THIS WAS HAPPENING, THE WOLF KEPT
EATING NON-STOP AND DIDN'T NOTICE WHEN
THE MAN APPROACHED.

SUDDENLY, THE MAN ENTERED THE KITCHEN AND CAUGHT THE WOLF EATING HIS PIECES OF MEAT.

WITHOUT THINKING TWICE, HE GRABBED A BROOM TO SCARE HIM AWAY.

WHEN HE RECEIVED THE FIRST BLOW FROM THE BROOM, THE WOLF TRIED TO ESCAPE THROUGH THE SAME HOLE HE HAD ENTERED THE KITCHEN.

HOWEVER, HE HAD EATEN SO MUCH THAT HIS BELLY GREW TOO BIG, AND HE GOT STUCK IN THE HOLE.

UPON SEEING THE WOLF STUCK, THE FOX SAID HE
WAS HARMING HIMSELF BY BEING GREEDY. THEN,
SHE LEFT HIM ALONE.

ON THAT DAY, SHE MANAGED TO GET RID OF THE WICKED WOLF AND LIVED HAPPILY EVER AFTER.

THE END.